For Tom Morrison (1944–1994)

Fireflies are not flies, but soft-bodied beetles. They have a luminous, light-giving organ that blinks on and off in the night to attract other fireflies. This light is a "cold" light; it does not give off any heat.

There are about 2,000 species of fireflies in the world, of which approximately 50 can be found in the United States.

Dear Parents:

Congratulations! Your child is taking the first steps on an exciting journey. The destination? Independent reading!

STEP INTO READING® will help your child get there. The program offers five steps to reading success. Each step includes fun stories and colorful art or photographs. In addition to original fiction and books with favorite characters, there are Step into Reading Non-Fiction Readers, Phonics Readers and Boxed Sets, Sticker Readers, and Comic Readers—a complete literacy program with something to interest every child.

Learning to Read, Step by Step!

Ready to Read Preschool–Kindergarten
• big type and easy words • rhyme and rhythm • picture clues
For children who know the alphabet and are eager to begin reading.

Reading with Help Preschool–Grade 1
• basic vocabulary • short sentences • simple stories
For children who recognize familiar words and sound out new words with help.

Reading on Your Own Grades 1–3
• engaging characters • easy-to-follow plots • popular topics
For children who are ready to read on their own.

Reading Paragraphs Grades 2–3
• challenging vocabulary • short paragraphs • exciting stories
For newly independent readers who read simple sentences with confidence.

Ready for Chapters Grades 2–4
• chapters • longer paragraphs • full-color art
For children who want to take the plunge into chapter books but still like colorful pictures.

STEP INTO READING® is designed to give every child a successful reading experience. The grade levels are only guides; children will progress through the steps at their own speed, developing confidence in their reading. The F&P Text Level on the back cover serves as another tool to help you choose the right book for your child.

Remember, a lifetime love of reading starts with a single step!

For Tom Morrison
(1944–1994)

Fireflies are not flies, but soft-bodied beetles. They have a luminous, light-giving organ that blinks on and off in the night to attract other fireflies. This light is a "cold" light; it does not give off any heat.

There are about 2,000 species of fireflies in the world, of which approximately 50 can be found in the United States.

Visit us on the Web!
StepIntoReading.com
rhcbooks.com

Educators and librarians, for a variety of teaching tools, visit us at
RHTeachersLibrarians.com

Library of Congress Cataloging-in-Publication Data is available upon request.
ISBN 978-0-593-43230-3 (trade) — ISBN 978-0-593-43231-0 (lib. bdg.)

Printed in the United States of America
10 9 8 7 6 5 4 3 2 1

This book has been officially leveled by using the F&P Text Level Gradient™ Leveling System.

STEP INTO READING®

world of
ERIC CARLE™

The Very Lonely Firefly

by Eric Carle

Random House New York

As the sun set

a little firefly was born.

It stretched its wings

and flew off into

the darkening sky.

It was a lonely firefly,

and it flashed its light

searching for other fireflies.

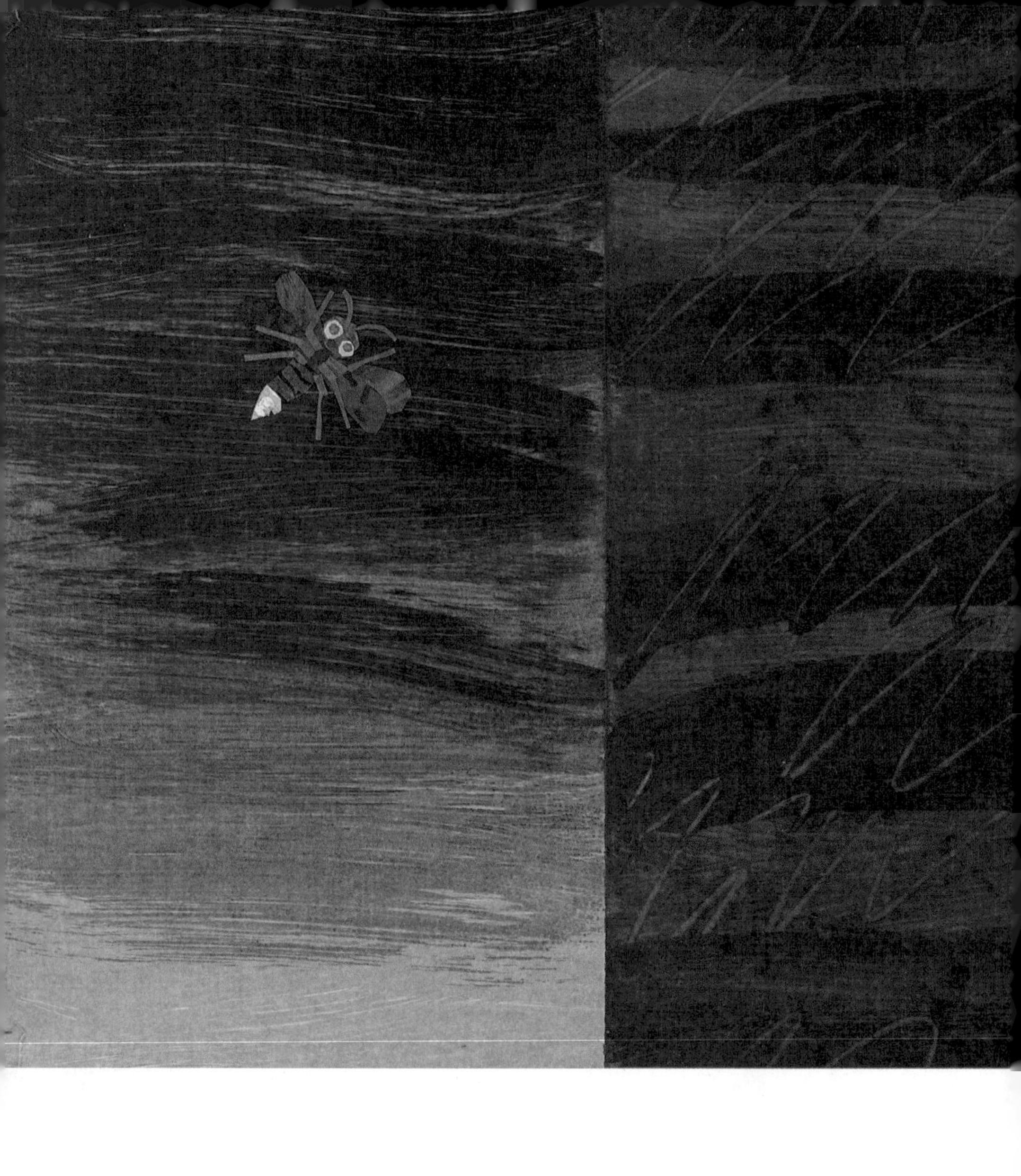

The firefly saw a light

and flew toward it.

But it was not another firefly.

It was a lightbulb

lighting up the night.

The firefly saw a light

and flew toward it.

But it was not another firefly.

It was a candle

flickering in the night.

The firefly saw a light

and flew toward it.

But it was not another firefly.

It was a flashlight

shining in the night.

The firefly saw a light

and flew toward it.

But it was not another firefly.

It was a lantern

glowing in the night.

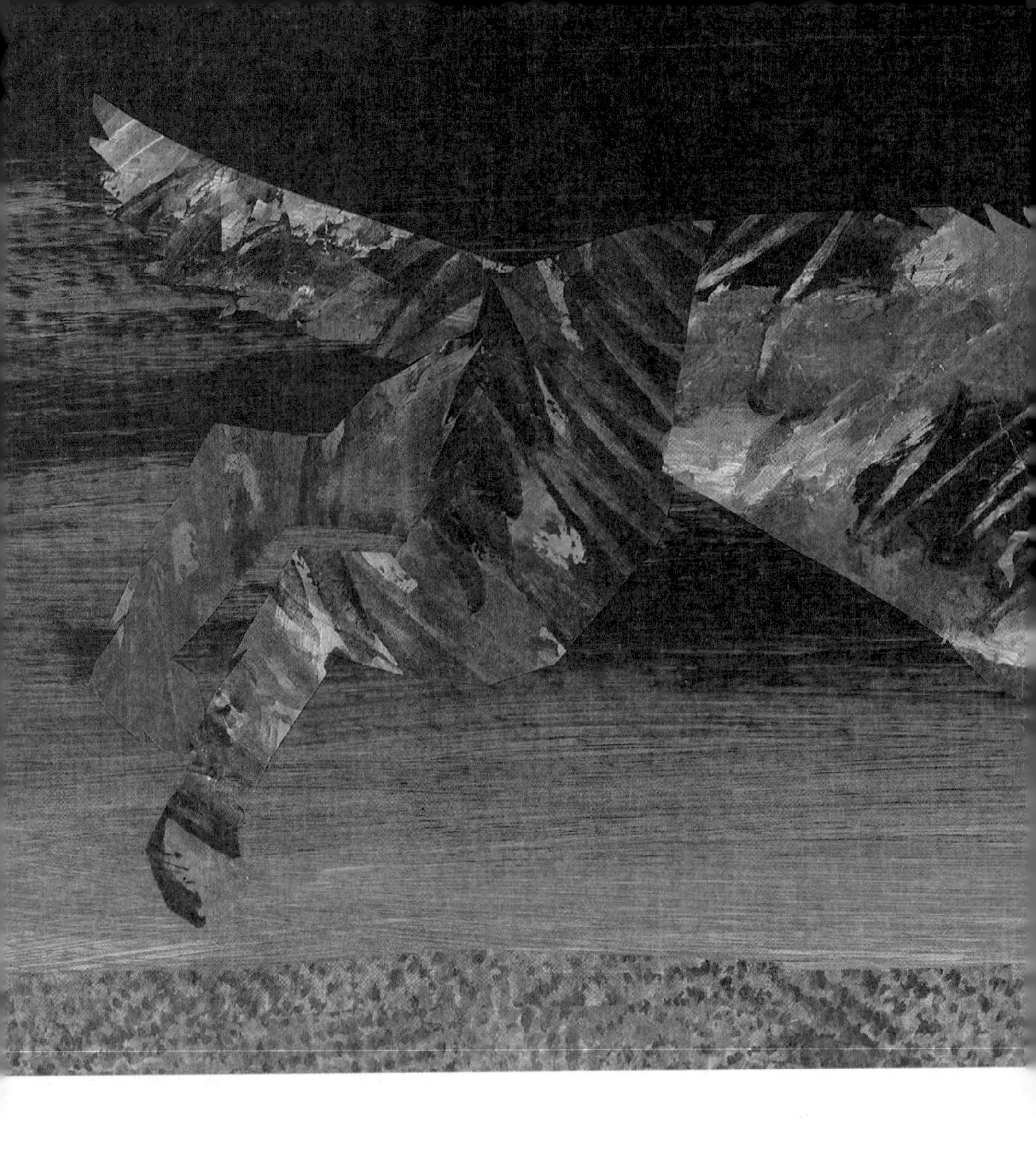

The firefly saw several lights
and flew toward them.

But they were not other fireflies.

There was a dog and...

a cat and...

an owl,

their eyes reflecting

the lights.

Hoot

The firefly saw a light

and flew toward it.

But it was not another firefly.

It was a car's headlights

flooding the night.

The firefly saw many lights

and flew toward them.

But they were not other fireflies.

They were fireworks

sparkling and glittering

and shimmering in the night.

When all was quiet,

the firefly flew through the night

flashing its light,

looking and searching again.

Then the very lonely firefly saw

what it had been looking for...

a group of fireflies,

flashing *their* lights.

Now the firefly wasn't

lonely anymore.